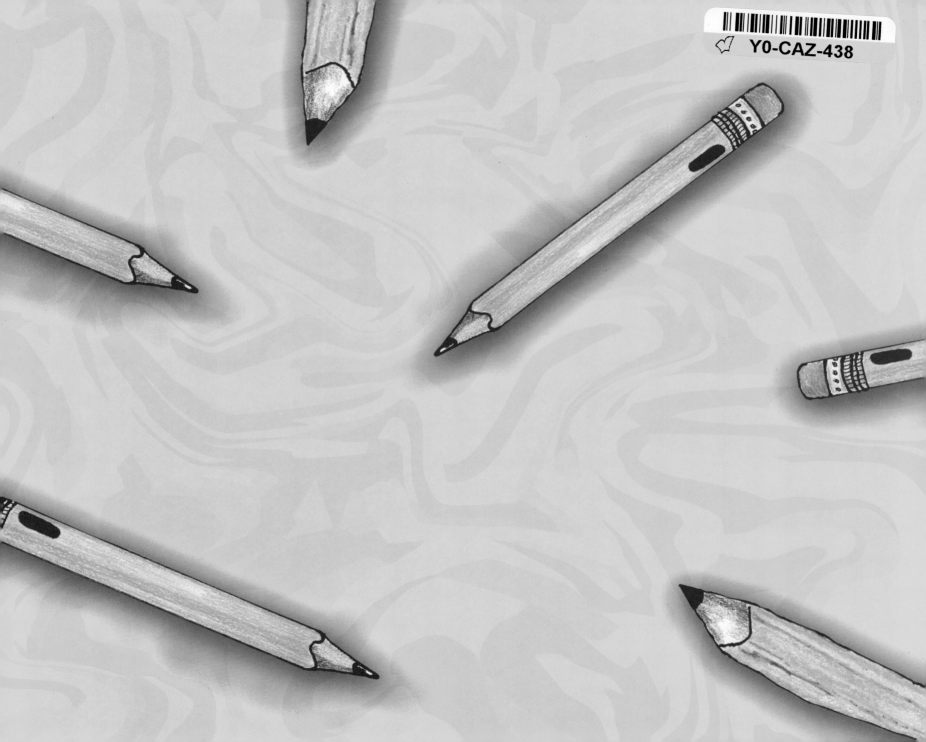

THE STUDENT FROM
Zombie Island

CONQUERING THE RUMOR MONSTER

WRITTEN BY MICHAEL J. MOOREHEAD

ILLUSTRATED BY KATHY PARKS

Five Star Publications, Inc. • Chandler, AZ

Linda F. Radke, President
Five Star Publications, Inc.
PO Box 6698
Chandler, AZ 85246-6698
480-940-8182

www.zombieislandbooks.com.

Publisher's Cataloging-In-Publication Data

Moorehead, Michael J.
   The student from Zombie Island : conquering the rumor monster / by Michael J. Moorehead; illustrations, Kathy Parks.

      p. : ill. ; cm.

   Summary: When the children hear that a new student, Bust 'Em Up Bill, will be joining their class, rumors begin to fly.
   ISBN-13: 978-1-58985-072-9
   ISBN-10: 1-58985-072-6

1. Rumor--Juvenile fiction. 2. School children--Juvenile fiction. 3. Rumor--Fiction. 4. School children--Fiction. I. Parks, Kathy Q. II. Title.

PZ7.M66 St 2007
[Fic]

Printed in Canada

Editor: Lynda Exley
Cover Design: Tanja Bauerle
Interior Layout: Tanja Bauerle
Illustrations: Kathy Parks
Project Manager: Sue DeFabis

The text of this book is set in Palatia.
The Illustrations were rendered in mixed media (colored pencil, chalk and ink pen).

ABOUT THE RUMOR MONSTERS

Rumor Monsters have huge mouths with which to blab and big ears to listen to gossip. Their heads are small and pointed because they have little brains and don't think about the consequences of what they say. Rumor Monsters travel in pairs because it takes two to start a rumor.

For Ms. Lujan, my second-grade teacher, for inspiring me to write.

- M. M.

WHAT OTHERS ARE SAYING...

"Michael J. Moorehead is a new generation Shel Silverstein! With humor and insight, his story (and the fantastic illustrations by Kathy Parks) will help young readers everywhere realize the absurdity of spreading rumors. This is an important message told in a way that kids will listen - and get it."

Paul M. Howey, author of
Freckles: The Mystery of the Little White Dog in the Desert
Asheville, North Carolina

Winter break is over, and kids are back in school. They say we are going to have a new student in our class today. His name is Bust 'em Up Bill. I wonder where he got that name? I hope he doesn't break all my pencils and crayons or bite the caps off of my markers!

I heard from Suzy Frederick that Bill comes from Zombie Island. He's 6 feet tall with scaly green skin, dragon-like claws, yellow fangs and a flaming red Mohawk.

Suzy says his breath is so bad it will singe your face if you get too close to him when he talks to you. If he burps near you, it might set your hair on fire!

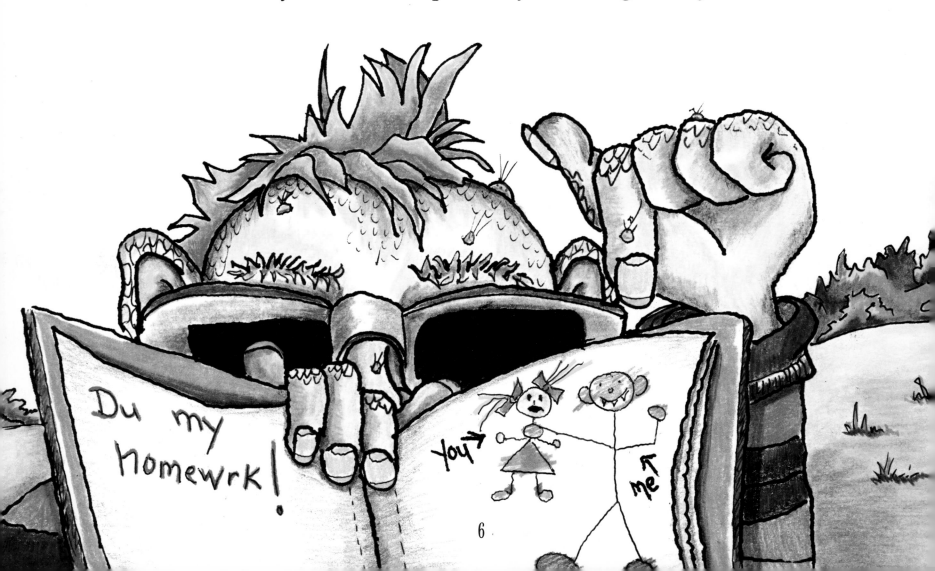

6

MAYBE I'LL WEAR A FIREPROOF HELMET TO SCHOOL TOMORROW.

Seth Green says Bust 'em Up Bill drives a monster truck. If our teacher, Ms. Lujan, gets in the way, Bill will blow his horn and blast her to the moon!

If there isn't a parking space, he will make one by crushing the cars with his huge tires and park on top of them. He doesn't even have a driver's license!

Instead of giving Ms. Lujan an apple on his first day, I bet he gives her an apple pie...

...SMACK IN THE FACE!

When Ms. Lujan turns her back to write on the blackboard, he will probably shoot rotten tomatoes at her with a slingshot.

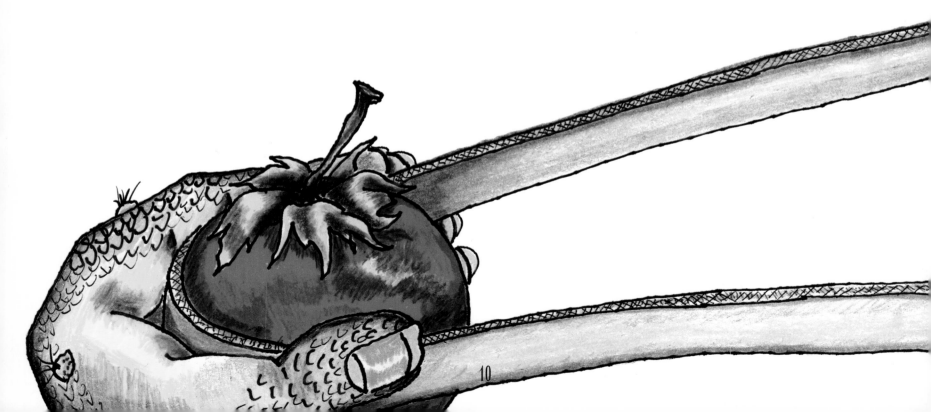

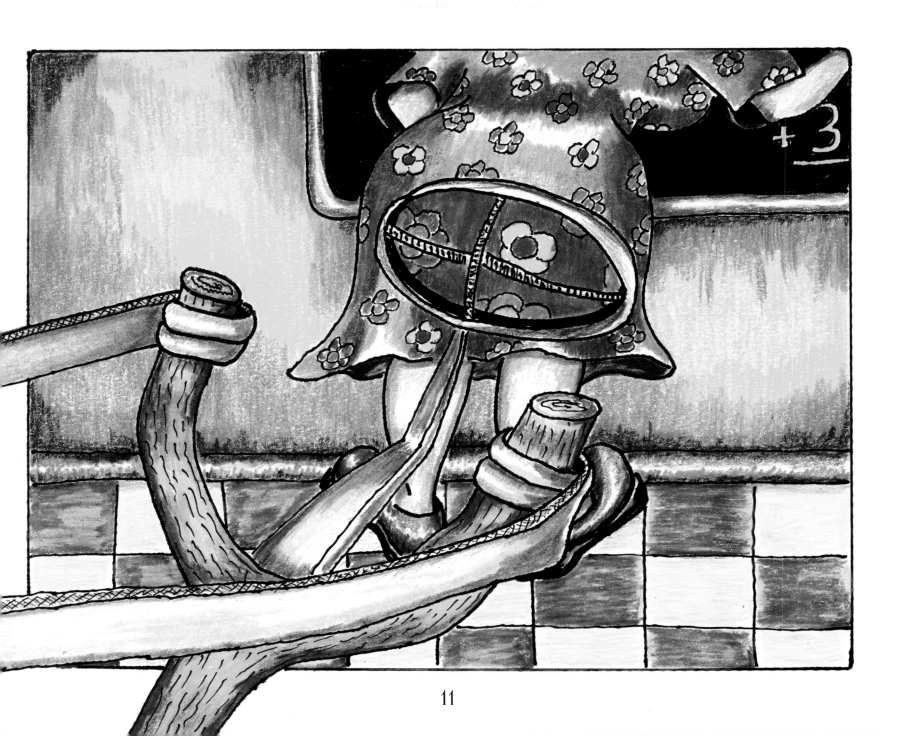

I'm dreading recess. Penny Jinx says at Bust 'em Up Bill's old school he made the kids act like monkeys on the monkey bars, eat unpeeled bananas and swing from their tails. I don't even have a tail. I'll probably fall off and swallow my retainer!

Playing on the swings is my favorite. Guess I won't do that any more. I'm afraid Bust 'em Up Bill will tie all the swings into a big knot -

...WHILE THE KIDS ARE STILL ON THEM!

13

Sammy Soso says he heard Bill has a laser gun he stole from the CIA. When the kids go down the slide, he uses them for target practice. If you refuse to go down, he zaps you with the laser gun and melts you into a yellowish liquid. **I HATE YELLOW!**

I better not play in the sandbox either. That would give him a chance to bury me in the sand. Nobody would know where I was because I'm such a pipsqueak. I probably wouldn't be dug up until summer vacation – **if they found me at all!**

I think I'll skip recess and stay in Ms. Lujan's class to do extra pages in my math book.

Sally Sanchez says at lunch time Bill sneaks into the classroom and puts whoopee cushions filled with chocolate pudding on every chair. I hope I remember not to sit down. If I do, it will look like I had an embarrassing accident.

I'm not going to let my lunchbox out of sight for a second. If I do, Tyler T. Tiger says Bust'em Up Bill will steal my sandwich and replace it with a knuckle sandwich - made with real knuckles!

When he eats, I heard Bust 'em Up Bill chews with his mouth open. Beth Bean's friend told her she saw a whole second-grade class in his mouth one day –

DESKS AND ALL!

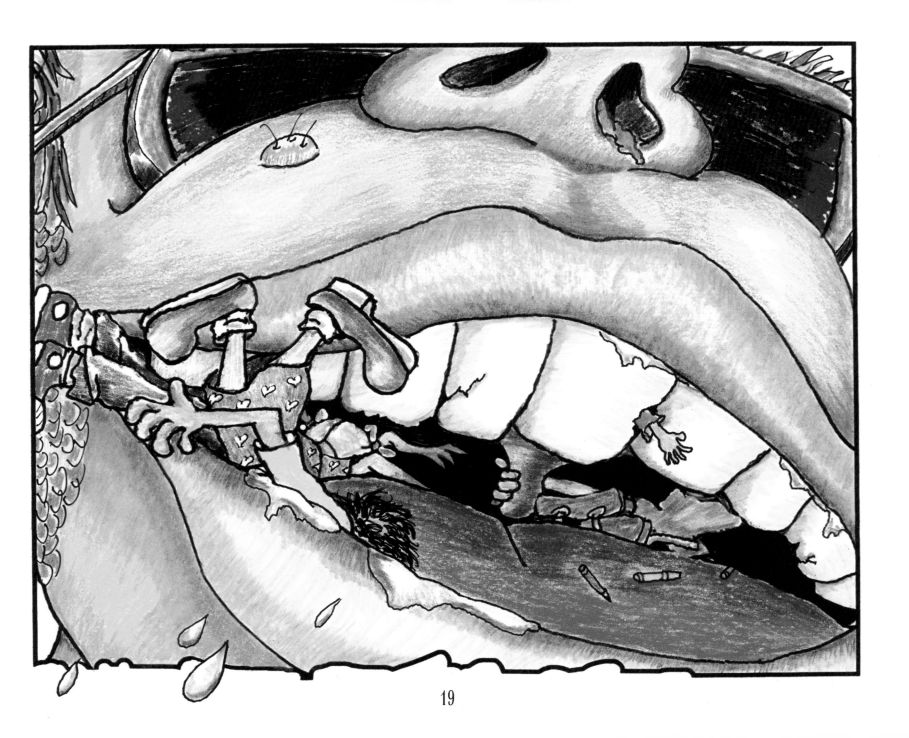

When Bust 'em Up Bill goes to gym class, T.J. McGravy says Bill doesn't do the exercises like the rest of the kids. Instead, he makes the gym teacher do them until he drops. Then Bill makes all the kids run around the track 5,000 times – sideways! I can't even run sideways!

T.J. says when Bill plays dodgeball, he uses bowling balls, and when he plays football, he uses real feet! I better keep my shoes on. Or better yet, I'll wear my dad's army boots.

I'm dreading music class. Tim Rock heard Bill's last music teacher quit because he flossed his teeth with the guitar strings and used drumsticks like chopsticks.

In
art class, I'm told he
likes to face paint the teacher
— with permanent paint — and give
her a new haircut with the scissors.
But that's not the worst part…

When the teacher isn't looking, he fills her
purse with vinegar and baking soda.
Then he blames it on the shortest kid
in the class. That would be...

ME!!!

During math, instead of crunching numbers, Willy McNilly says Bust 'em Up Bill crunches all the light bulbs. Then you have to do math in the dark.

I hope I don't have to sit next to Bill in a dark room. He might accidentally bite my head off. And I need my head to do math!

We're supposed to have a spelling bee today. George McHenry says Bust 'em Up Bill doesn't know how to spell, so he brings real bees to class.

I hope I don't get stung! I'm allergic to bees, especially spelling bees. If a bee stings me, I'll swell up like a giant watermelon! Today is going to be the worst day of my life!

Oh, no! The bell just rang, and school is about to begin. I can hear footsteps moving toward Ms. Lujan's class! Bust 'em Up Bill is late. Maybe he will pass the classroom and keep going out the exit at the end of the hall!

No such luck! I can see the doorknob turning. My heart is pounding so loud, it sounds like a time bomb.

I think my head is going to explode into a million pieces!
The door is opening … It's Bust 'em Up Bill and there's something red in his hand.

It's… it's… it's…

Oh My Gosh!!!

... an apple???

"Here, Ms. Lujan. I'm looking forward to being in your class," says Bill. "They call me Bust 'em Up Bill, because I like to make my teachers laugh."

At lunchtime, Bill gets an extra spoon and shares his chocolate pudding with me.

Day Spa Treatment

CHOCOLATE

Put Tomatoes And Green Stuff Here

He picks up extra trash off the floor and smiles at the cafeteria lady when he hands her back a perfectly clean tray.

During gym class Bill shows me how to throw a really long pass with the football. After class, Bill and I help the teacher put away the balls.

Out Of Bounds

Time Out NOT my job!

When music class rolls around, Bust 'em Up Bill plays the drums like a legendary rock star. I love drums. They're my favorite!

36

In art class, Bill draws a comic strip using the kids in the class as the characters. It's so funny even the teacher laughs.

Now I understand why they call him
Bust 'em Up Bill!

The school day is over and Ms. Lujan thinks Bust 'em Up Bill will be one of her favorite students. I think he will be my new best friend. I'm so glad Bust 'em Up Bill came to my school. I hope he's in my class next year, too!

ABOUT THE AUTHOR   Michael J. Moorehead

When **Michael J. Moorehead** isn't writing, he's hiking, baking oatmeal cookies, playing video games and participating in Boy Scouts. His favorite animal is the polar bear, and he hopes to one day become an environmentalist. He's concerned about the plight of the polar bears and says he wants to stop global warming to save the majestic white creatures from extinction - but he will have to graduate from junior high school first. Michael lives in Tempe, Arizona, with his mother, a freelance writer and editor for the *SanTan Sun News* and *Arizona Parenting* magazine, and his father, an insurance property adjustor, who moonlights as a movie critic for the *Wrangler News*.

ABOUT THE ILLUSTRATOR   Kathy Parks

Kathy Parks was quite content being a loving mother and accomplished amateur athlete, until she developed a neuromuscular disorder that left her weak and with tremors. Recalling how much she'd enjoyed art in high school, she began to dabble in batik, and soon had customers lining up to buy her creations. An injury to her hand caused her to switch from batik to drawing and painting, giving way to a new career as an illustrator. Kathy's muscles still tremble a bit, and she often has to put weight on her drawing hand to keep it still, but her spirit - and certainly her creative talents - remain undaunted. She lives with her husband and children in Phoenix, Arizona.

ABOUT THE PUBLISHER   Linda Radke

Publisher **Linda Radke's** enduring passion is for children. With the introduction of Five Star Publication's new imprint, Little Five Star, she will capitalize on her training in childhood education (she holds degrees in Education, Special Education and Elementary Education) to support childhood literacy. Linda has 20-plus years of publishing experience demonstrating her unwavering commitment to helping authors publish their works, and has garnered numerous book awards along the way. Linda was recently named "Book Marketer of the Year" by Book Publicists of Southern California.

Little Five Star's mission is to help authors create books that will help children understand the implications of their life choices and help them become more tolerant and accepting of the differences in people.